-My Family-
My
Single Mom

by Claudia Harrington
illustrated by Zoe Persico

Looking Glass Library

An Imprint of Magic Wagon
abdopublishing.com

To my grandparents that always give me unconditional love, even with every change of hair color. —ZP

abdopublishing.com

Published by Magic Wagon, a division of ABDO, PO Box 398166, Minneapolis, Minnesota 55439. Copyright © 2018 by Abdo Consulting Group, Inc. International copyrights reserved in all countries. No part of this book may be reproduced in any form without written permission from the publisher. Looking Glass Library™ is a trademark and logo of Magic Wagon.

Printed in the United States of America, North Mankato, Minnesota.
052017
092017

 THIS BOOK CONTAINS
RECYCLED MATERIALS

Written by Claudia Harrington
Illustrated by Zoe Persico
Edited by Heidi M.D. Elston
Art Directed by Candice Keimig

Publisher's Cataloging-in-Publication Data

Names: Harrington, Claudia, author. | Persico, Zoe, illustrator.
Title: My single mom / by Claudia Harrington ; illustrated by Zoe
    Persico.
Description: Minneapolis, MN : Magic Wagon, 2018. | Series: My family
Summary: Lenny follows Kenneth for a school project and learns what it's like to
    live with a single mom.
Identifiers: LCCN 2017930508 | ISBN 9781532130205 (lib. bdg.) |
    ISBN 9781614798354 (ebook) | ISBN 9781614798422 (Read-to-me ebook)
Subjects: LCSH: Family--Juvenile fiction. | Family life--Juvenile fiction. | Single-
    parent families--Juvenile fiction. | Mothers--Juvenile fiction.
Classification: DDC [E]--dc23
LC record available at http://lccn.loc.gov/2017930508

As the last bell rang, Miss Fish's second graders jumped out of their seats.

"Wait, Lenny!" Miss Fish handed him the class camera. "You're going home with Kenneth today. He's Student of the Week."

"Cool," said the boys.
Click!
"How do you get home?" asked Lenny.

Kenneth tossed a handball in the air. "We hang out with the after-school club for a while, then Mom will pick us up. They have great snacks!" Lenny's stomach growled. "Excellent!"

After snacks were inhaled, the leader supervised math homework. "Who checks your homework?" asked Lenny.

"Annie does," said Kenneth. "Annie, is this right?"

"Super," said Annie.

Click!

"What do you do now?" asked Lenny.

Kenneth wiggled his fingers. "I'll warm up my phalanges then beat you at handball!"

"You're on!" said Lenny. "But first, let's race across the monkey bars!"

When they got to the end, Kenneth swung up to the platform. "Fire pole!" He wrapped his legs around it and slid down.

"Excellent!" said Lenny, using the slide. "You look like a pro."
"My uncle is a firefighter," said Kenneth. "I hang out with him when Mom has to work late."

Kenneth grabbed the handball. "Ready to play?"

"Sure," said Lenny. "Do you want to play with any special rules?"

Kenneth smiled. "How about watermelons?"

Lenny made a face. "Is that where you have to duck under the ball before it hits you?"

Kenneth laughed. "Well, before it bounces on the ground."

"Maybe just regular," said Lenny.

When the score was tied, a woman in a lab coat walked up to Kenneth.

"Are you sick?" asked Lenny.

Kenneth doubled over. "Meet my mom.

She's a pediatrician."

Click!

"You must be Ace Reporter Lenny," said Kenneth's mom, leading them to the car.

Lenny's cheeks burned.

Soon, they pulled into a driveway.

Click!

"Here we are," said Kenneth's mom. "If homework is done, you boys may play until dinner."

The boys high-fived.

"Hope I didn't hurt your pha-LAN-ges!" said Lenny.

Kenneth grabbed the handball and bounced it over. "You first."
Lenny rubbed his hands together and served.

"Ow! Good one!" said Kenneth, rubbing his forehead.

"Oops," said Lenny. "Who gets your ice pack?"

Click!

Kenneth laughed. "Mom does. It's her specialty. But it just grazed my frontal bone, so I don't need it."

Lenny carefully took his next turn.

Then, Kenneth's serve flew onto the neighbor's roof.

Click!

Kenneth grinned. "I do that a lot."

"Who gets your ball down?" asked Lenny.

"Watch this," Kenneth told Lenny as he aimed their hose at the ball.
Click!

"Wash up for dinner, boys," called Kenneth's mom as the wet ball bounced down. "And splashing doesn't count."

Lenny laughed as they went inside. "Who makes your dinner?"
"Mostly Mom," said Kenneth. "It's just the two of us. But I help!
Too late for pigs in blankets, Mom?"

Lenny made a face.

Kenneth snorted. "Don't worry. It's just wrapped up turkey dogs."
Click!

When dinner was over, Kenneth showed Lenny his room.

"Wow!" said Lenny. "Who gave you that?"

Click!

Kenneth patted the skeleton's head. "Mr. Rattles? Mom got him in med school. I can name almost all the bones!"

"Cool," said Lenny. "I think I know, but who taught you?"

"Mr. Rattles!" joked Kenneth. "And Mom. I might be a doctor, too, when I grow up!"

Kenneth's mom kissed his head bump.

"Lenny, your mom's here."

When Lenny's mom came in, Lenny

asked Kenneth, "Who tucks you in?

Mr. Rattles?"

"Ha-ha," said Kenneth. "His hugs are too bony, but Mom's are the best. Then she quizzes me on body parts."

"I think I know this, too," said Lenny. "Who loves you best?"

Both moms smiled and hugged their boys. "We do!"

Click!

Student of the Week

Kenneth

"See you tomorrow, handball newbie," said Kenneth. "Tomorrow, handball oldie," said Lenny. "BONE up on handball, Mr. Rattles!"